The Wizard of Oz

Written by Abie Longstaff

Illustrated by Louise Pigott

Collins

1 The Cyclone

"Dorothy!" Uncle Henry threw open my bedroom door. "Wake up! There's a cyclone coming! Get to the shelter!"

I gasped and jumped out of bed.

"Dorothy!" I heard Aunt Em's voice through my window. She was standing in the farmyard, holding the storm shelter door open. "Hurry!" she cried.

Across the fields, I could see a dark twisting tower of wind racing towards me.

"Toto! Toto!" In a panic, I called for my dog.

Aunt Em was waving frantically. "Leave the dog!" she yelled over the wind.

No way! Toto was my best friend. Uncle Henry had bought him for me when I came to live with them in Kansas, after my parents died. I loved him with all my heart.

"Toto!" I shouted again. Desperately, I searched my room until I found him shaking with fear under the bed.

"Toto! Come here!" I couldn't reach him. I looked up at the black sky. Tears prickled my eyes. I couldn't leave Toto behind. What was I going to do?

All at once there was a terrifying

whoosh!

My stomach felt as if it had dropped out of my body. The house had lifted into the air! That was the last thing I remembered before the enormous bang.

2 Munchkinland

Bang!

Our house landed on the ground. My head was sore, but I was alive!

I felt a lick on my hand. "Toto! There you are! Let's go and find Aunt Em and Uncle Henry!"

But when I opened the front door, Kansas had gone. Before me was a strange land with blue hills and an orange river.

"Where are we?" I whispered, clutching Toto.

A group of very short people approached me. With them was a tall woman, dressed in sparkly white robes.

"Welcome to Oz!" she smiled, and a warm glow spread over me. "I'm the Good Witch of the North. My friends here are the Munchkins."

The short people bowed. "We thank you for killing the Wicked Witch of the East," they said solemnly.

"Who, me?" I was shocked. "I've never killed anyone!"

The Good Witch pointed to two feet in silver slippers sticking out from underneath my house.

"I'm so sorry!" I gasped. "It was an accident."

"She was bad," the Good Witch explained. "She made the Munchkins her slaves."

"You freed us!" the Munchkins cheered.

My mind was spinning. Witches? Munchkins? If this was a dream, I wanted to wake up right away!

"Do you know the way to Kansas?" I asked hopefully.

The Good Witch frowned. "I've never heard of Kansas. This is the Land of Oz. You must go to the Emerald City and ask the Great Wizard of Oz for help. He knows everything."

The Good Witch waved her wand. The feet under the house melted away, leaving only the pair of silver slippers behind.

"These slippers will take you where you need to go," she said. "They are very powerful. Follow the yellow brick road to the Emerald City, but watch out for the Wicked Witch of the West."

Another evil witch? A shiver went down my spine as I set off down the yellow brick road.

3 The Yellow Brick Road

It felt odd to be wearing a dead witch's shoes. My Aunt Em said you can get used to anything if you try. But I don't think she was talking about magical slippers.

Soon Toto and I saw a scarecrow in a field. Birds were pulling bits of straw out of his ears. Toto barked to chase them away.

"Thank you!" cried the scarecrow.

"A talking scarecrow!" I exclaimed in surprise. "That's very strange."

"Is it?" asked Scarecrow.

"Well, yes," I said, "but I don't come from Oz. Many odd things happen here, don't they?"

"I don't know," Scarecrow said. "The farmer only made me this morning and I haven't been given a brain."

With that, I remembered my manners. "I'm Dorothy. I'm going to ask the Wizard of Oz to help me get back home. He knows everything."

"Wouldn't it be wonderful to know everything?" sighed Scarecrow. "Do you think this wizard could give me a brain?"

"Maybe," I replied. "Let's ask him together."

Arm in arm, we hopped and skipped our way down the road until we came across a shiny silver statue of a man. I heard a squeak from inside him.

"Oh!" I cried. "I think the statue is alive! He's a man made of tin!"

Seeing a nearby oil can, Scarecrow poured some oil into the tin man's joints.

The tin man started to move. "Thank you," he said. "I've been stuck for ages. My tears made me rusty."

"Why were you crying?" I asked.

"Because I haven't got a heart," replied Tinman sadly.

"Then come with us to the Great Wizard of Oz," Scarecrow said. "He'll give you one. He knows everything."

So off the three of us went, down the yellow brick road.

4 The Dark Forest

Before long, we came to a forest. My heart started beating faster as a growl between the trees became a roar!

Out leapt a huge lion. He knocked Scarecrow and Tinman over, then he ran after Toto!

"Stop that, you bully!" I shouted at him.

To my surprise, the lion stopped. Then he burst into tears!

"I'm sorry!" sobbed Lion. "You scared me as you walked by."

"Why would a great big lion like you be scared of us?" asked Scarecrow crossly, as he stuffed straw back into his body.

"I'm scared of everything. I haven't got any courage," said Lion.

Scarecrow still looked annoyed, but Tinman patted Lion kindly.

"Why don't you come with us to see the Wizard of Oz?" said Tinman. "He knows everything. He could give you some courage."

So three became four, and off we went.

Lion really was scared of everything, especially witches. "The Wicked Witch of the West has terrible powers," he whimpered. "She can turn people into stone! She even has a flock of flying monkeys!"

Poor Lion; he trembled all the way to the Emerald City.

5 The Emerald City

There, at the end of the yellow brick road, shone the glittering spires of the Emerald City. We'd made it! All we had to do was find the wizard, and our wishes would come true.

We ran straight up to the bright green gates.

"We're here to see the wizard," I told the guardsman.

He frowned. "No one can see the wizard," he said.

"But why? We've come so far. You must let us in!" My voice shook in frustration. I couldn't give up now.

"Let Dorothy in!" said Lion bravely. "She killed the Wicked Witch of the East!"

"Accidentally," I added quickly.

"Look," said Scarecrow, "she's wearing the witch's silver slippers!"

Clever Scarecrow; that did the trick!

"All right," said the guardsman, "follow me." He led us across the busy city and into a green marble Throne Room.

We gasped in amazement. The Wizard of Oz was a huge floating head!

"Speak!" the wizard boomed.

Each of us told the wizard what we needed: a brain, a heart, courage and a way back home.

"I'll grant your requests," the wizard answered, "but only if you kill the Wicked Witch of the West!"

"I can't kill a witch!" I said with a sob of despair. "Not on purpose anyway." I buried my head in my hands. Tinman gave me a creaky hug.

"Don't worry, Dorothy. I'll think of something," said Scarecrow anxiously.

Lion took a deep breath. "If Dorothy is to get back home, we have to face the witch."

6 The Wicked Witch

My heart sank when I learnt where the witch lived: right in the middle of the Dark Woods, miles away from the Emerald City.

That night we walked and walked, over hills, rivers and fields and into the Dark Woods. We were so tired, but we had to go on. Deeper and deeper we went, cutting our way through the spiky branches, until, finally, we reached an iron gate. A stone castle towered over us, tall and sinister.

My heart was pounding. We were all so scared we nearly turned back. But Tinman took my hand, and Lion cautiously pushed open the gate.

I jumped with fright as cobwebs brushed my face.

We tiptoed into the silent courtyard filled with statues of creatures. Suddenly there was a whoosh and the Wicked Witch of the West swooped towards us on her broomstick. Her eyes burnt like fire. "Get them!" she shouted. "They'll all be my slaves!"

Creak!

The witch's flying monkeys grabbed my friends with their strong arms. As the monkeys dragged them away, the witch turned her terrible eyes on me.

"Run, Dorothy!" Lion shouted bravely. "Save yourself!"

"Ahh, Dorothy!" she glared at me. "It was you who killed my sister! You'll work hardest of all." She threw a mop and bucket at me.

Brave Toto barked and ran at the witch to protect me.

"I'll turn you to stone, you horrible dog!" The witch laughed cruelly as her wand began to crackle and spark.

I looked around frantically for a weapon, for anything I could use to save Toto. The witch lifted her wand higher.

Without thinking, I grabbed the bucket of water and threw it at her as hard as I could.

"Arghhh!" she screamed. "No! Not water!"

The witch began to shrivel up. Her body shrank down until she melted away in a cloud of green smoke.
Then she was gone.
I couldn't believe it!

"Hooray, Dorothy!" said Scarecrow. "You've killed the witch!"

"Accidentally," I replied. "Again."

The flying monkeys bowed before us. "By killing the witch, you've freed us from her evil spell. What can we do for you in return?"

"Please take us back to the Emerald City," I asked. "We have to see the wizard right away!"

7 The Wizard of Oz

Thanks to the flying monkeys, we were soon standing before the Great Wizard of Oz again. We were so excited that our wishes were about to be granted!

"Speak!" the wizard boomed.

"We've done as you asked," I proudly announced. "The Wicked Witch of the West is dead. Now you must help us."

The wizard went quiet for a moment. "I can't," he admitted.

"Wh… what do you mean, 'can't'?" my voice wobbled. I turned to my friends. They looked as confused as me.

The wizard boomed again, "Leave the presence of the mighty Oz!"

"Wait!" I cried in desperation. "You have to help us!"

Suddenly, Toto ran forward, grabbing the wizard by his scarf. As Toto pulled, the scarf fell away to reveal a little man in a large basket. He was holding a megaphone and his huge head was not a head at all! It was a hot-air balloon with a face painted on it.

"You're the mighty Oz?" said Scarecrow slowly. "You tricked us!"

"I'm sorry," said the small man. "I had to pretend to be a wizard to keep the witches away."

He began to untie the ropes that held the balloon to the ground.

"Where are you going?" I called as the balloon rose into the air.

"Now the witches are dead, I'm not needed here anymore," he said.

"But what about my brain?" said Scarecrow.

"My heart?" said Tinman.

"My courage?" said Lion.

"You all already have everything you need," the wizard called down. And with that, he disappeared from sight.

8 The Silver Slippers

"The wizard's gone!" cried Scarecrow.

"He left us!" said Tinman.

"What shall we do?" asked Lion.

I thought about what the wizard had said. "He's right!" I realised. "Scarecrow, it was you who put oil on Tinman's joints to free him. That was clever!"

Scarecrow nodded, thinking.

"Tinman, you were kind to Lion even when he scared us. You have a huge heart," I said.

Tinman smiled.

"And Lion, you faced the Wicked Witch of the West, even though you were the most afraid of her. That's real courage."

Lion puffed out his chest with pride.

"But what about what you need, Dorothy?" asked Tinman, kindly.

I shook my head sadly and looked at the floor. As I did, I remembered what the Good Witch had told me: "The slippers will take you where you need to go."

"The slippers will take me home!" I exclaimed happily. "But –" tears filled my eyes – "I'll… I'll never see you again."

I hugged my friends tight.

"We'll miss you!" they cried.

"I'll never forget you," I promised. I picked up Toto and tapped my heels together one, two, three. "Take me home!"

9 Home

There was a whirling mist. Lights flashed before my eyes. I felt myself being lifted up…

Next thing I knew, I was back in Kansas!

Before me was a brand new farmhouse. Uncle Henry was putting in the last window. Aunt Em was painting the front door.

"Aunt Em! Uncle Henry!" I cried. Relief swept over me: I'd made it home!

"Dorothy!" They shouted with joy and lifted me up into their arms.

"We thought we'd lost you," said Uncle Henry. "We missed you so much."

"I missed you too. I'm so happy to be back!" I hugged them.

"Well," said Aunt Em, "there's no place like home."

That's true, I thought, snuggling down in my bed that night with a contented sigh, but there's certainly no place like Oz either.

Ideas for reading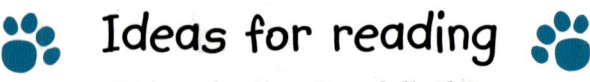

Written by Clare Dowdall, PhD
Lecturer and Primary Literacy Consultant

Reading objectives:
- discuss words and phrases that capture the reader's interest and imagination
- draw inferences and justify these with evidence
- make predictions from details stated and applied

Spoken language objectives:
- ask relevant questions to extend their understanding and knowledge
- give well-structured descriptions, explanations and narratives for different purposes

Curriculum links: Geography - climate

Resources: ICT for research and voice recording, art materials

Build a context for reading

- Explain that *The Wizard of Oz* is a famous story that has been made into a film, and that this book is a retelling of the story.
- Look at the front cover and ask children to tell you what they know about the story already. Help children to name the characters and describe their qualities as far as possible.
- Read the blurb aloud. Ask children to predict how Dorothy might find her way home in this version of the story.

Understand and apply reading strategies

- Turn to pp2–3 and read the chapter heading "The Cyclone". Check that children know what a cyclone is and what happens in one.
- Read p2 to the group. Help children to make inferences about Dorothy's character and life story, asking questions as necessary. List her qualities on a whiteboard.